Lynne Rae Perkins

Clouds for Dinner

Greenwillow Books New York

Pen and ink and watercolor paints were used for the full-color art.

The text type is Bookman.

Greenwillow Books, a division of William Morrow & Company, Inc.,

1350 Avenue of the Americas, New York, NY 10019.

Printed in Hong Kong by South China Printing Company (1988) Ltd.

First Edition 10 9 8 7 6 5 4 3 2 1

Library of Congress Cataloging-in-Publication Data

Perkins, Lynne Rae.

Clouds for dinner / by Lynne Rae Perkins.

p.   cm.

Summary: It takes a visit to her aunt's house
to make Janet appreciate her parents
and their unusual way of looking at everything.

ISBN 0-688-14903-0 (trade)

ISBN 0-688-14904-9 (lib. bdg.)

[1. Parent and child—Fiction.]   I. Title.

PZ7.P4313C1   1997   [E]—dc21   96-36898   CIP   AC

THIS STORY IS FOR LUCY.

anet had a mother who liked poems. Her mother liked paintings, too, and listening to music. She was always telling Janet and Harry to look at something or listen to something or smell something.

"Look at the golden light on those hills," she would say.

"Look at those gorgeous pink clouds."

"They're not really pink," Janet would answer. "You just think they're pink because the sun is on them."

"Look at those gorgeous clouds that I only think are pink," her mother would say.

Janet's dad said these things, too. He would take
a bite of melon and say, "Taste this. It's like eating
a cloud."

Clouds came up a lot where Janet lived, and when
they did, Janet's mother and father always had
something to say about them.

"Wow, those are amazing clouds," her mom would say.
"That one looks just like a Great Lakes freighter!"
her dad would say.
"Did we eat dinner yet?" Janet would ask. Not
because she was hungry, but because dinner
was not always easy to recognize at Janet's house.
It was clear enough when they all sat down at the
table together. But some days they would be eating
apples and bits of cheese or muffins, and by and by
nobody was hungry anymore. And that was dinner.

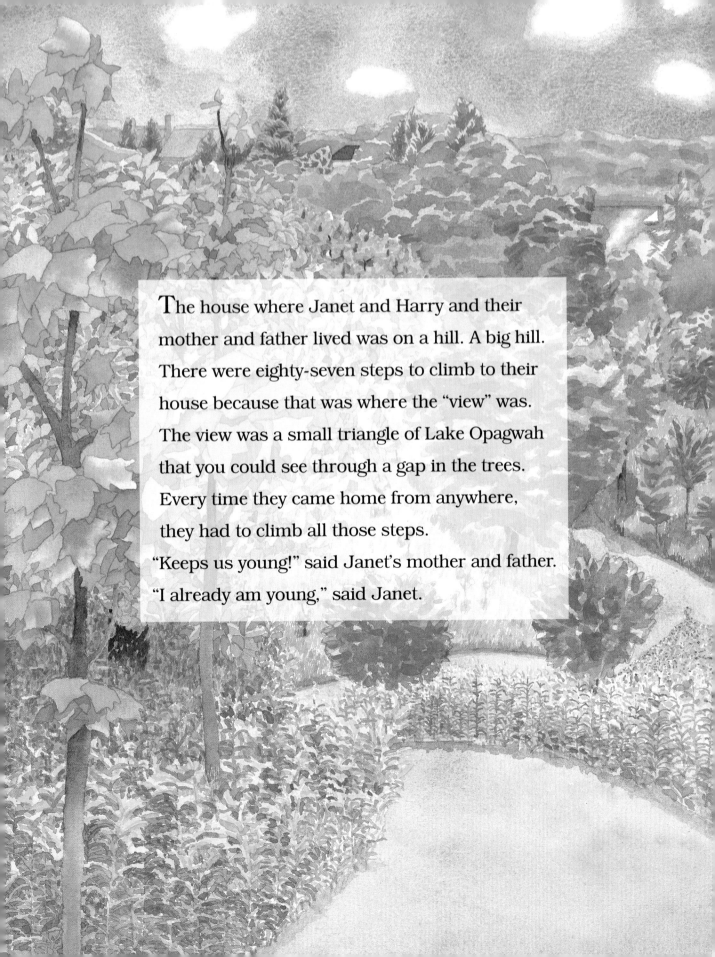

The house where Janet and Harry and their
mother and father lived was on a hill. A big hill.
There were eighty-seven steps to climb to their
house because that was where the "view" was.
The view was a small triangle of Lake Opagwah
that you could see through a gap in the trees.
Every time they came home from anywhere,
they had to climb all those steps.
"Keeps us young!" said Janet's mother and father.
"I already am young," said Janet.

She thought they should live in a sensible house
like Aunt Peppy and Uncle Tim's, where the
front door was only two steps higher than the
driveway. And where dinner was unmistakably
dinner. Not to mention, where the beds were
always made, the dishes were always washed,

and there was a TV room with chairs that
flipped back until you were almost lying down.
Janet was delighted when Aunt Peppy and
Uncle Tim invited her to spend a weekend at
their house.

She had a wonderful time. There was so much going on.
Uncle Tim gave the dogs a bath, and he let Janet do the
rinsing with a hose.

Aunt Peppy was getting ready for a big party.
Janet helped her fill paper cups with colored
mints and tie netting around them with ribbons.
Janet's cousins let her play with them, even though
they were older and even though they were boys.

In the afternoon the cousins had a soccer game. Janet sat in the bleachers between Uncle Tim and Aunt Peppy and cheered.

On the way home they drove through the car wash.
And that was just the first day; those were just the
special parts. Even the regular things were
great, like listening to Aunt Peppy
answer the phone,
which rang a lot.
She was so—peppy!

Three times a day they all sat down
together for a big, noisy meal.
"I wish I lived with you all the time,"
Janet told Aunt Peppy.

Aunt Peppy laughed, and hugged her,
and kissed her on top of her head.
"Kids always think that about their
aunts," she said.

On the second morning of her visit Janet woke up early,
so early that it was still dark, except for a wedge of pink
at the edge of the sky. The noisy house was quiet now, asleep.
Janet sat up in the unfamiliar sofa bed, with the different
blankets pulled up over her shoulders. Her back was chilly.
She watched the pink light spread slowly, and now there
was apricot, now turquoise, now lavender.

The trees were almost black against the sky.
A breeze stirred the branches, and a handful of leaves
was blown into the air. The leaves sprouted wings,
turned into birds, and flew away.
They were birds all along, of course, but they had

looked like leaves at first, and it seemed as if something magical had happened.

Janet wanted to tell someone about it. She wanted to run into the next room and jump on her parents' bed and tell them, but she wasn't at home and her parents weren't in the next room.

So she told Aunt Peppy at breakfast.
But Aunt Peppy didn't get it. "What woke you
up so early?" she said. "I hope it wasn't the dogs.
Do you want some more toast? You boys settle
down, now. Is the paper here yet, Tim?"
"It was cool, Aunt Peppy," Janet said.
"I knew I should have given you another
blanket," said Aunt Peppy. "Okay, everybody,
let's clear the dishes and get a move on."
Janet started to miss her mother and dad
and even Harry. And their house on the hill.
Not that she wasn't still having fun. She went
into the TV room to ride the recliners.

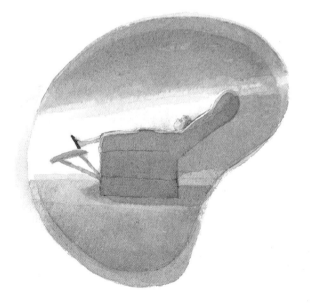

That evening, during the drive back home, Janet thought
of the leaf-birds, and she told her mother about them.
"Wow," said her mom. "What a lucky thing to see. I wish
I'd been there."
"Me too," said Janet. She felt happy to be riding in the car
with her mother, happy to be going home.
A last bit of sunlight shot across the fields and turned
the hills to gold. Above them the clouds looked like a place
where a person might really be able to walk.
Then it was dark.
"Aunt Peppy makes a big dinner every night," said Janet.
"Everybody sits down together. It's really fun."
"I know," said her mother. "Which part do you like?
The big-dinner part or the sitting-down-together part?"
"Both parts," said Janet.

The car's headlights lit up round amber-colored
reflectors on mailboxes and driveway markers.
A few times they lit up the eyes of deer standing
in the fields, or trees near the road.

From a distance it was hard to tell which was
which, and Janet's mother slowed down each
time until they were sure.
They were almost home now.

"I guess I like the sitting-down part," said Janet.

"Oh, good," said her mom, "because that part
sounds good to me, too."

The car slowed to a stop and they got out.

The eighty-seven steps rose before them in
the moonlight.

"Dang!" said Janet's mother. "That hill is
still there!"

"Keeps you young," said Janet.

"Oh," said her mom. "That's right. Last one
up is a rotten egg."

And that very night, even though it was a little late, Janet
and Harry and their mother and their dad sat down
at the table. Anyone could tell this was dinner.